Lessons

from

Liberty

Rebekah A. Morris

Cover design by Rebekah A. Morris

ISBN: 9798832945002

Read Another Page Publishing

Dedication

To our Founding Fathers, who gave their lives, their fortunes,
and their sacred honor to secure our liberty.
And to every patriotic American, young and old, who loves their
country.

Acknowledgements

A big thank you to Sarah Holman for inviting me to be a part of
the *A Very Bookish 4th of July* collection. I so loved getting to
write a full story centered around one of my favorite holidays,
and I've enjoyed being a part of the team.
To my mom, for coming up with the perfect name for the ice
cream store, titling my book, and for all her editing and
proofreading. I couldn't have done it without you, Mom!
Special thanks to Abigail Harris for all her help with the Air
Force lingo, and for answering my odd questions about things.
Lastly, I have to say thanks to Angie Thompson for writing the
perfect synopsis for this story. I still don't know how you do it,
Angie, but you make me want to read my own books.

CONTENTS

1.
Eight Cousins

Twelve-year-old, Liberty Goldman burst into the kitchen one bright June morning, a book in one hand and a pair of sunglasses in the other. "When's he coming, Mom?" she asked, dropping her book and sunglasses on the table and sitting down for breakfast.

Mrs. Goldman didn't turn from the counter where she was cooking pancakes on the griddle. "Dad? By mid-July."

"No, I meant Alec."

"Today."

Liberty sighed. "I meant when today?"

"Honey, if you want a specific answer to a specific question, it's better if you ask that question at the start." Mrs. Goldman glanced over her shoulder at her second daughter. "And you know the rules. No books at the table."

With a quick, "Oops, sorry," Liberty picked up her book and carried it into the living room and set it down on a shelf. "There," she said, with a fond pat to the cover, "I'll eat breakfast quickly and then we can go outside. Alec is coming today."

"Libby, breakfast!" Avery's voice called her.

Skipping back to the kitchen, she found her four sisters beginning to seat themselves at the table. It was Dory's turn to ask the blessing and Liberty bowed her head.

"Dear Jesus," Dory prayed, "thank You for this food. And thank You for Saturday. And please bless Daddy and bring him home soon, soon, soon. Amen."

"Amen," Liberty echoed. She glanced up the framed family picture hanging on the wall. It was her favorite picture, for it had been taken last year on the 4th of July which was also her birthday. Daddy had his Air Force tee-shirt on and was holding Jainy in one arm; his other arm was around Mom, while the other girls were gathered around in their matching patriotic summer dresses and holding flags in their hands. Now Daddy was away on deployment. He'd been gone for nine months already and had one month left.

"Libby," Mom said, "I'm not sure when Alec is supposed to arrive. Aunt Tessa said she thought he'd be coming after lunch, but it might not be until supper time."

Attacking her stack of pancakes, Libby grinned. "When he comes we'll be the book only backwards!"

"What book?" Avery asked.

Liberty swallowed her bite. "*Eight Cousins*. You know, Rose goes to live with her uncle and– Mom! Rose lives with her Uncle Alec, and Alec's name is the same!" Libby squealed.

"But how is it backwards, Libby?" eight-year-old Nan wanted to know.

"Because Rose had seven boy cousins, and Alec has seven girl cousins."

"Which Alec? The story one or our cousin?" Nan

questioned before stuffing a large bite of pancake into her mouth.

"Our cousin. You should read the book, Nan."

Nan shook her head. "Ish do pig."

"Nan," Mom chided, "wait until your mouth isn't full, please."

"I know what she said, Mom," Liberty remarked. Nan's dislike of reading anything that looked long was well known. "But we will be like the book. Avery is Archie—"

"I am not Archie." And Avery stared at her younger sister with her best 'big sister' look. Avery was fifteen and very much a girly girl, hating to get really dirty, and keeping her blonde hair long so she could wear it in curls for special occasions.

Not daunted, Liberty went on as though she hadn't been interrupted. "We even have Jainy instead of Jaimie. I wonder what Alec will be like."

"I don't know, but you'd better finish eating before the flag raising."

With the energy Liberty put into most things she did, she concentrated on her breakfast.

The dishes would have to wait, for breakfast had taken longer than usual, and the flag raising couldn't wait. Thankful it was summer and they didn't have to wear shoes, Liberty skipped outside after her sisters. She raced Nan and Dory up the grassy hill to the flag pole at the top. This was one of Liberty's favorite times of the day.

Mom, Avery, and Jainy came up the hill a little more slowly with the flag folded neatly. Liberty helped Avery attach the flag to the clips and then stepped back, for it was Dory's turn to hold the flag so that it wouldn't touch the ground.

A bell in the church across the lake's inlet began to ring, and with its first notes Avery began to pull the flag up to the top of the flag pole. The breeze off the lake caught its bright colors and snapped it straight out.

Liberty's hand went to her heart as her eyes fastened on the Stars and Stripes above them. She joined the rest of her family in saying the pledge, and only after it was over did she let her eyes travel along the shore of the lake. From her place on the hill, she could count at least a half a dozen flag poles all proudly flying Old Glory. "Please, Lord," she prayed silently, "be with Daddy right now and keep him safe."

"Come on, Libby," Avery said, touching her sister's arm. "We have to go clean up the kitchen. Then we'll get Summer and Piper and go over to Grandma's to help get ready for Alec."

"All right. Race you to the house!" Liberty took off down the hill with her sister right behind her.

In no time the dishes were washed, the floor swept, and the girls, even Jainy, were heading out into the bright sunshine with sunglasses perched on their nose, flip-flops on their feet, and hair up in high ponytails to keep it out of the way. Liberty carried her book in one hand on the chance that she would have a few minutes to read.

"You're a grand old flag, you're a high flying flag," Avery broke out into song as the girls marched up the hill.

"And forever in peace may you wave." The others joined in the song lustily, keeping step quite well. They sang the entire song as they marched along the lake shore past the first house where the McGuires lived, then past the Reed's house, and stopping before the third house where they were joined by their cousins

Summer and Piper.

"Does your mom know when he's coming?" Liberty asked Piper as they started off again.

Piper shook her head, her own blonde ponytail flipping across her shoulders. "I think this afternoon. What book are you reading now?"

"*Eight Cousins.*"

"Didn't you just read that?"

"Yes, but it's my favorite book, or one of my favorites. Did you realize that we'll be a backwards version of it? Instead of seven boy cousins, Alec is coming to seven girl cousins. And we've never met."

"But his parents aren't dead, they just live in other countries all the time because of Uncle Dawson's business, and he's going to live with Grandma and Grandpa instead of some aunts," Piper said. "Alec is, I mean."

"I know," Liberty sighed. "And we don't have an unmarried uncle. Or an aunt."

"That's okay," Piper consoled, "it's still fun to pretend. Have you gotten to talk to your dad lately?"

Liberty shook her head. "Mom has gotten some emails from him, but we haven't gotten to Skype or anything. She said we might get to tomorrow though." Looking around, she suddenly noticed that they had slowed down during their talk. "Come on, we'd better catch up with the others."

Grandma and Grandpa's house was set on a hill overlooking a wide sandy beach and the placid waters of the lake. Nearly every house in their lakeside community overlooked the lake at least a little bit. Boats were used almost if not more than cars were, and the main street of town ended at a pier where folks docked their boats to go shopping.

The girls ran up the sandy hill and onto the green grass which was Grandpa's pride. He kept it mowed, watered and fertilized, dug up any dandelions which dared poke up their heads, and collected the pinecones which fell from the ancient pine tree across the road and traveled into Grandpa's grass.

Liberty and Piper, hand in hand, reached the back porch first and raced up the steps, the others right behind them. Bursting into the kitchen, Liberty pushed her sunglasses onto her head as she called, "Grandma, we're–" She stopped suddenly, staring at the boy sitting at the kitchen table eating breakfast.

He looked up and for a moment stopped chewing.

No one said a word for several seconds until Grandma bustled in. "Well, you girls arrived sooner than I thought. I had just called your moms to say that Alec had arrived last evening."

"I thought he wasn't coming until today?" Liberty said, still staring at her cousin who had returned to his breakfast.

"We all did until your grandpa realized we had the dates wrong. You know Alec had to cross the International Date Line from Japan, and we thought it was Saturday our time which was Sunday their time, but it was really their Saturday and our Friday."

"I'm confused," Nan said.

"So am I," the newcomer said, laying his napkin on the table and standing up. He was tall and blonde, with a friendly smile and twinkling blue eyes. "I might have seen pictures of the seven of you, but that was different because you were always in the same place in the pictures, but now I don't know who is who."

"Line up," Avery ordered.

Liberty couldn't quite keep back her smile as she

took her place. Avery didn't know how much she acted like Archie sometimes.

Alec came around the table. "What is this, a review?"

"Oh, they always do that, Alec," Grandma said. "With Grandpa and now your Uncle Byron in the Air Force, a little military style creeps into everyday life. You'll get used to it. Now, I'll leave you all to get acquainted while I go water my geraniums."

Alec hesitated a moment as though unsure where to start. Then he moved to the head of the line. "You must be Avery." He held out his hand.

"Yes. Welcome to Silver Lake, cousin." And Avery shook hands with a smile before Alec moved on to the next cousin.

"I'm Summer. Piper and I are sisters. Did you have a good trip?"

"Yep, even though it was long."

Liberty was next and she grinned up at her cousin. "I'm Liberty, but you can call me Libby, or Lib, or Libs. I'll answer to just about anything. Do you like to read?"

"Hi. Yes, I do like to read. Do you?"

"She's the family book worm," Avery said.

"I can't help it if I like to read more than the rest of you." And Liberty shrugged.

"I'm Piper, and I try to keep Libby from getting too lost in books."

"Pleased to meet you, Piper."

"I'm Nan, and she's Dory," Nan said, introducing herself and her sister. "We're not twins 'cause I'm nine and she's eight, but I'm as small as her."

Alec shook hands and said it was nice to meet them both. Then he crouched down in front of the last girl. "You must be Jainy because I know there is a Jainy, and since no one else has claimed that name, it must be you."

Jainy giggled and nodded.

"How old are you, Miss Jainy?"

"Five."

"That's a really good age. You don't have to go to school like the older kids, but you can still learn. And you aren't a baby any more, but you are still young enough for people to read stories to you and carry you when you get tired."

Liberty looked at Piper and raised her eyebrows. She didn't think boys knew how to make friends with little kids. But, she had to admit, Jainy was easy to be friends with.

Straightening back up, Alec looked at the girls and then asked in puzzled tones, "What do I say to make you all into normal cousins again instead of military offspring?"

"Just say 'dismissed' or 'break ranks'," Liberty offered. "That's what Dad and Grandpa say."

"Dismissed!"

2

Just Another Day

Everyone started talking at once, asking questions which no one answered, giving instructions which no one heard, and telling stories which no one listened to.

Catching sight of Alec's confused expression, Liberty put her hands over her ears and shouted, "Throttle back!"

Everyone stopped talking and then turned to look at her.

"If we all keep talking at once, we're going to scare our cousin right back to the airport, or at least up to his room where he can hide from us like Rose hid from her cousins."

Avery was the first to speak. "Sorry, Alec. We can all take turns talking, but we don't always do it. If we get too crazy, just say 'throttle back' like Libby did and we'll quiet down. It's an Air Force thing." She shrugged and turned to Summer. "Shall we go find out if Grandma needs our help with anything?"

The two girls departed arm in arm.

Alec grinned. "My mom sent presents. They're in the living room and have your names on them."

That sent Nan, Dory, and Jainy out of the room, leaving only Liberty and Piper behind with Alec.

"How old are you?" Liberty asked, hoping he wouldn't be too old though he was tall.

"Fourteen. Is that too old?" A twinkle sparkled in his eyes and his lips twitched in a smile.

"I guess not. But Rose was only thirteen when she arrived." She held out her beloved book. "Have you read *Eight Cousins* before?"

Sitting down in a chair, Alec took the book and flipped through it a minute. "I think I have. It seems sort of familiar."

Piper gasped. "You have? But it's about a girl. I thought only girls read it."

"Piper," Liberty exclaimed, "there are seven boys in it, and Uncle Alec, and Uncle Mac, and oh—others."

Still slowly flipping pages, reading a bit here and there, Alec asked, "Do you all play you are the seven cousins?"

"No, but some of us are rather like them," Liberty admitted. Seeing the interested look on her cousin's face, she said, "Let's go out on the deck and I'll tell you."

"Sound good to me. I haven't been outside yet except when I arrived, and then it was kind of dark." And Alec rose and pushed open the screen door, nodding for Liberty and Piper to go before him. "What a great view!" He crossed the deck and leaned against the railing. "It looks like everyone is getting ready for the 4th of July."

"Huh? Where? Why?" And the girls ran over to stand beside him, looking eagerly for signs of the holiday which was still several weeks away.

"The flags. I don't think I've ever seen so many

American flags all at the same time before."

"Oh, those are always up," Liberty said, somewhat disappointed. "Almost every house on the lake has one, and when the bell rings each morning, everyone puts theirs up. Well, some people leave their flag up all the time 'cause they have a light on it. We don't. We like putting it up every morning. We say the Pledge of Allegiance after we put it up too. Weren't you up this morning when Grandma and Grandpa put their flag up?"

Alec shook his head. "Nope. The time change has me so mixed up that I guess Grandma didn't want to bother me." Turning around, he perched on the railing. "Now what?"

"Well," Liberty began, but she got no farther for the screen door opened and Grandma appeared with Avery and Summer.

"Suppose you girls take Alec and show him about the place," Grandma said. "He's going to be here for a few months and should know the way around. Go on now." She shooed them off the porch.

"What about the younger ones?" Liberty asked as they crossed the green grass and headed down to the sand.

"Grandma said they could stay there," Avery answered. "Alec, I hope you brought better shoes than those for walking around. If you wear tennis shoes you'll get sand in them and it will take days before it all comes out."

Alec looked down. "Uh, nope. I guess I need to get something."

"Let's take him to town to get something else to wear," Summer suggested. "Otherwise he won't have as much fun." She looked at him. "Do you have any money on you?”

Alec shook his head. “No, but I can run back to my room and get some.” When the girls all nodded, he turned and loped back to the house.

“I think I’m going to like him,” Liberty remarked. “Maybe he’ll help us decorate the boat for the parade.”

“Let’s ask him! I’m sure Dad will be happy for another guy to help.” Piper pulled her scrunchie out, flipped her head upside down and redid her ponytail.

Staring up at the flag fluttering in the breeze, Liberty gave a little sigh. “I wish Dad could be back for the 4th.”

“I’m sure he does too, Lib,” Avery said, putting her arm around her sister’s shoulders. “It’s hard to have a birthday without Dad home.”

Liberty knew her sister understood at least a little of what she was feeling, even if it wasn’t quite the same. It wasn’t just him not being home for her birthday, it was Dad being gone for the holiday they both loved so much. “Maybe we can Skype with him that day.”

“I’m sure he’ll try to at least call and talk to you,” Avery assured. “Here comes Alec.”

“Here I am again. Lead on and I’ll follow.” His bright face and merry eyes awakened answering smiles from the girls, and they set off for town.

“Alec,” Piper asked, “do you want to help us decorate our boat for the parade on the 4th?”

“Your boat? I’ve heard of floats in a parade but never boats. Is it a real boat or just made to look like one?”

Liberty pushed her sunglasses up on her forehead so she could stare at her cousin. “Of course it’s a real boat. We have a boat parade. Everyone decorates their boats and we go all around the lake. It’s much more fun than walking down a blistering hot street."

"As long as you don't fall out of the boat," Alec remarked with a bit of uncertainty in his voice.

"Oh," Summer said easily, "if you do, the next boat will pick you up."

"Hmm," was all the reply Alec gave.

They reached the town, and the girls led him straight to a small shop. A bell jingled as they stepped inside, and Liberty waved to someone behind the counter. "Hi Mrs. Sten. This is our cousin Alec. He's just arrived and needs flip-flops so he doesn't ruin his shoes in the sand. And–" She turned and looked up at Alec. "Do you have sunglasses? No? Then you'll need some of those too unless you want to go around with black patches under your eyes looking like a ball player."

"And Uncle Byron says that won't help much with the lake," Piper added.

Alec shrugged. "I guess I need sunglasses too then."

It really didn't take long before Alec was outfitted with sunglasses and flip-flops. Tying his shoelaces together, he stuffed his socks into his shoes and hung the shoes over his shoulder. "Where to now, cousins?"

The girls showed him the few most important places in town: the church, library, diner, and the bank.

"Come on, let's go inside and say hi to Dad," Piper suggested. "He works at the bank, you know," she added for Alec's benefit.

"He doesn't usually work on Saturdays," Summer put in, "but sometimes he does."

Uncle Hunter was delighted to see his nephew and greeted him warmly.

Back on the street again, Avery glanced at her watch and said, "We should hurry back so Alec can meet

Aunt Tessa and Mom before it's lunch time."

"Let's run," Liberty suggested.

"Hey, there's no way I can run in these flip-flops," Alec said. "It's hard enough trying to walk in them. I feel like a little kid wearing my dad's shoes."

"You can take them off as soon as we get to the sand. That's what we often do." And Liberty led the way out of town to the sandy beach near the water.

They removed their shoes and the group made their way around the lake. Liberty could tell their cousin wasn't used to going barefoot for though he didn't say anything, he winced and picked up his feet as though the warm sand burned them. "You can walk in the water," she told him. "It feels good in the summer." She watched with satisfaction as Alec followed her suggestion. "Maybe we can go swimming this afternoon."

"Swimming?" Alec's voice was hesitant and uncertain.

"The little girls would want to come, Libs," Avery said, turning and walking backwards a little bit.

"I know, but maybe Mom would let them if Alec came with us." She looked up at him. "Do you want to go swimming this afternoon?"

"Um—" He didn't answer because the three younger girls came running down from Grandpa's grass, their arms full of the presents Aunt Stacie had sent.

Grandma called from where she stood by the flag pole. "Alec, just go along with the girls. Aunt Jo will feed you lunch. Summer, Piper, your mom is over at Aunt Jo's."

"Thanks, Grandma!" Summer called back, waving.

"Come on, let's fly," Nan said. "I want to show Mom my things."

The cousins raced along the sandy shore, across yards where there was no sand, and arrived at last behind the brown, two story house. There Alec was hugged and welcomed by both his aunts, and everyone sat down for lunch.

"Mom, if Alec goes with us, could we all go swimming this afternoon?" Liberty asked before crunching a chip.

Her mom hesitated. After a quick look at Alec, she shook her head. "Not today. Alec is still probably suffering from jet lag, and it wouldn't be a good idea for him to go swimming."

Though Liberty was disappointed, she didn't argue. It wasn't like there wouldn't be plenty of time to go swimming.

*

"Did Alec arrive okay yesterday?" The voice was a little scratchy coming over the speakers. It was Sunday afternoon and the family was having a Skype call with Dad.

"He came on Friday, Dad," Avery said. "Grandpa and Grandma got the date mixed up because of the International Date Line."

"We like him, Daddy," Nan put in, bouncing in her seat. "Me and Dory do."

"And me too!" Jainy, eager not to be left out, shouted.

Dad chuckled. "That's good. What about you, Libs, do you like him too?"

Liberty nodded. "He likes to read, Dad, and he said he thinks he's read *Eight Cousins*!"

"Another book lover, huh? That's nice."

"When are you coming home, Daddy?" Liberty asked, hoping he'd say by her birthday.

"I don't know for sure, honey. Middle of July is all I can tell you. If you all get some fireworks, save them until I get home, and we'll shoot them off together, all right?"

"Okay."

"I have to go now. I love you all!" And Dad blew a kiss to each girl and to Mom. "God keep you all until we meet again."

With many shouts of "Bye Dad!" and "Love you!" the call ended.

3.
Tears and Sunshine

Somehow Liberty felt like crying. She had hoped and hoped that Dad would say he'd be home for her birthday, but it hadn't happened. "Mom," she asked softly so the others wouldn't overhear, "I left *Eight Cousins* at Grandma's yesterday. Can I go get it? Please?"

Mom looked down and hugged her. "Yes. But take the cell phone, okay?"

Not trusting herself to speak, Liberty nodded quickly and ran to the shelf where the flip phone the girls carried when out and about was kept. Snatching the phone and shoving it into her pocket, she grabbed her sunglasses and a moment later was outside. She ran up the hill to the flag pole.

A warm summer breeze sent the flag fluttering merrily against the deep blue sky while an intense pain of fear, sadness, and longing sank deep into Liberty's heart.

With a sharp intake of breath, she hurried down the slope to a sheltered hollow and dropped to the ground. She pulled her knees up, folded her arms on top of them, and burying her face in her arms, she burst into tears. She loved her country and was so proud of her dad, but that didn't help the pain in her heart when he was gone. Great sobs shook her shoulders and tears spilled uncontrollably. "Daddy. Daddy!" She cried as she hadn't cried for a long time. It was as if all the tears she hadn't shed when they had said goodbye, and the tears she'd held back at night when she missed her father's hug and kiss, all demanded a release. She cried until her sobs grew quieter though the tears kept flowing.

"Libby?" The voice was hesitant, concerned.

Keeping her face hidden in her arms, she hiccupped, "W–what?"

"Are you hurt?"

She shook her head. Someone sat down beside her, but she didn't move, for she didn't want Alec to see her tear stained face.

"Did you get bad news about your dad?"

"He . . . he's not going to be here for my birthday!" The tears started again.

Alec patted her back. "I'm sorry. That must be hard, but hasn't he missed some of the other girls' birthdays?"

Trying to swallow back her tears, Liberty nodded her bowed head. "Yes. B . . . but it's not the same!"

"Why not?" Alec's voice wasn't condemning, only puzzled.

"B . . . because it's the 4th of July! A birthday you can celebrate later and it's okay, or . . . or he can be on Skype as you o . . . open your presents and blow out your candles, but you c . . . can't change the 4th of July, and he . . . he loves it, and he w . . . won't be home, a . . . . and we can't celebrate it l . . . later." The last few words ended in a little cry. Liberty knew she'd lost any esteem her cousin might have had for her, but right then she didn't care. The pain and hurt were too deep. Even Christmas could be postponed until a later date, she realized, or they could Skype opening presents. But not the 4th of July. Not Independence Day with its games, and boat parade, its food and speeches, costumes, excitement and fireworks at the end.

"Libby," Alec's voice was quiet, and there was no reproach in his voice. "I came to bring your book back to you. You left it at Grandma's yesterday."

Liberty let one arm down, though she tried to keep her face hidden as she fumbled for her pocket in hopes that she had a tissue in it.

"Here." A red bandana was pushed into her hand. "It hasn't been used. I don't know why I carry one around."

Mumbling, "Thank you," Liberty tried to dry her eyes, and then blew her nose.

Alec resumed talking. "I'm kind of glad you left it, because I read it. It was fun to read again. I was probably seven or eight the last time I read it. Mom had it on her shelf, and there wasn't much else around I could read, so I read *Eight Cousins*. I'd forgotten a lot of it. Don't tell the other girls, but I think I'm a little bit like Rose."

Pushing her sunglasses over her eyes so Alec couldn't see how red they were, Liberty turned and looked at her cousin. "Like Rose? No, you're not."

"Oh, yes I am. You see, I've never been on a boat, and I'm a little afraid of getting on one. And I can't swim. I never learned how because I've always disliked cold water unless it's to drink."

"Oh."

"But if I'm to help decorate a boat for the parade, I'll have to get over that fear, won't I?" He smiled and then frowned. "Libs, I'm afraid there are a great many things I don't know. I'm going to need a lot of help. I've lived so much of my life in other countries that I'm rather out of place in my own. It's a strange feeling." He stretched his long legs out in front of him and leaned back on his elbows. "Here there are American flags flying everywhere I look. I hear talk of boat parades, fireworks, races, and I don't know what, but to me the 4th of July is–now don't disown me, cousin– just another day on the calendar."

"But it's not!" And Liberty straightened up. "It's the birthday of the greatest nation in the world. It was founded on the belief that man had the right to obey God and serve Him as he saw fit, not how some king or queen decided. Our Founding Fathers risked everything so that we could have a say in the laws which govern us, in how we live, what jobs we do, and who our leaders should be. It's not just because we broke away from England, it's about freedom, and liberty, and oh, so much more!" She looked at Alec. "We'll have to start your education soon."

"I guess so."

For several minutes the two cousins sat in silence soaking in the sunshine and the summer breeze.

At last Alec pushed himself up. "I should get back to the house before Grandma begins to wonder."

"Thanks for bringing my book back."

"My pleasure. And Liberty, I think your dad would want you to celebrate the 4th of July just as if he were here. If he's fighting for freedom, don't you think he'd want you to celebrate that freedom?"

Liberty watched Alec walk away across the grassy

hill until he disappeared down the other side. She knew he was right. "Daddy would want us to celebrate the 4th just as we always do," she murmured with a sniff. Absently, she picked up the book Alec had brought back to her. "He's going to have a lot to learn before the 4th of July. Perhaps Uncle Hunter could teach him to swim. After he gets used to the water."

Opening the book in her hand, Liberty's eyes fell to the pages, and she soon forgot everything else in the beloved story of Rose and her seven cousins.

*

The water of the lake felt very refreshing that summer afternoon. Liberty had coaxed Alec to come join them all in a swim. "We won't really go swimming," she had told him, sitting cross-legged on Grandma's back porch. "There's a place where the sand goes out quite a ways, and even Jainy can go with us there. Come on, please! You have to learn to like the water if you're going to swim. Mom's going to be there too, and Aunt Tessa."

Alec had given in with a half rueful look. "It's hard to refuse you, Libby. I suppose I'll have to learn sometime and—"

"It might as well be now." Her smile was contagious.

So he had joined the girls and his aunts in the walk around the lake until they were almost directly opposite the town. A wide sandy beach sloped gently down into the water. The girls had dropped their towels in the sand, kicked off their flip-flops, and headed straight into the water. But Alec hesitated.

Liberty couldn't see his eyes behind his sunglasses,

but she guessed he was either scared or still disliked the idea of cold water. "Take your flip-flops off," she ordered, planting her hands on her hips, the bright blue of her swim skirt blowing about her knees and giving her a very patriotic look with her red and white striped shirt.

"Why?" Alec didn't move.

"Because the sand is so hot you'll want to walk in the water."

Drawing a long breath, Alec followed her directions and somewhat to his own surprise, was soon in the water with the others.

"See," Liberty managed to whisper to him, "it's not bad in the lake, is it?"

"You're right. It's not what I was expecting." He looked across the gleaming water. "Do people ever swim across the lake?"

"Oh, yes. Daddy does when he's home. Avery did it with him last year. And he said I could try it this year if I wanted to. I think I might. Do you want to do it too?"

"I don't even know how to swim, remember?"

"But you're going to learn. Now that you like the lake it won't be so hard. If Uncle Hunter doesn't have time, ask Grandpa."

Alec tossed the beach ball back to Jainy. "I thought Grandpa was in the Air Force not the Navy."

Refraining from rolling her eyes, Liberty said, "And what happens if the plane crashes at sea?"

Splashing after the ball he had failed to catch, Alec sent it back to Jainy and waded back. "I guess I hadn't thought of that. I should have. I flew over enough water on the way here." He grinned down at his cousin. "You'll just have to put up with my ignorance in all manner of things, Libs. I'm farther behind on my American education than I thought."

"We'll teach you. Come on, it looks like Avery and Summer are going back to the beach. Let's go dry off and eat lunch. Nan, Dory!" Liberty called, "Let's eat lunch!"

The picnic lunch on the sandy beach was lively. Talk was constant and ideas for decorating their boat for the 4th of July parade were tossed around; then they tried to explain Patriotic Charades to Alec.

"We always play it the morning of the 4th," Piper said, putting a white sun hat on her head to shade her face. "It helps the morning go by faster. We'll have to come up with new words this year, Aunt Jo."

"I'm thinking of some, Piper," Aunt Jo said with a smile.

"I want Alec on my team," Liberty announced.

Alec flopped back on his towel with a groan. "Do you want to lose, Libs? Remember I'm not good with all that patriotic, red, white & blue, Founding Fathers lingo. It's going to take me months to get ready for the 4th of July! All this talk of games, decorations, and activities has made me hungry again." He sat up. "Is there anything left?"

Avery opened the lunch cooler and looked inside. "Yep, an extra sandwich, one picnic egg, and one slice of watermelon." She looked at him. "What do you want?"

"Everything."

Dory's eyes widened as the last of the food was passed over. "How does he eat so much?" she whispered to Nan.

Aunt Tessa laughed. "Jo, I think we're going to have to start packing food as though our husbands were with us. Or more."

"That's why I packed extra. I grew up with brothers." And Aunt Jo smiled at Alec.

Liberty scooped up a handful of sand and let is trickle through her fingers. "We need to plan the food for Independence Day."

Alec choked on his sandwich and stared at her with wide eyes. "There's another day?" he asked in mock horror. "What happens on that day?"

"It's the same day," Summer said. "The 4th of July *is* Independence Day. Sometimes we call it one name, sometimes another." She shrugged and smoothed her pink swim skirt.

"Well, that's a relief. I think." And Alec stuffed the entire picnic egg into his mouth at once. Chewing it thoughtfully, he stared down at the rest of the sandwich in his hand. When his mouth was empty, he remarked, "I think I need a notebook to keep track of all the American things I'm learning." He lifted his sandwich and then looked over at Liberty. "What were you saying about food?"

Liberty giggled. "We have to plan our food for the big celebration."

4.

To Sunville

"Grandpa," Liberty said, walking beside him over the green grass looking for dandelions. "Won't you take Alec and me out on the boat soon? He's never been on one and is kind of scared of them. I know he doesn't know how to swim yet, but couldn't we go anyway?"

Stopping, Grandpa bent and dug up the bright flower which had dared to grow in his green grass. "I might. We could take all the girls–"

"Oh, please no!" And Liberty shook her head quickly. "Just us two. You see," she leaned closer to her grandfather and whispered, "Alec doesn't want the others to know he's scared of boats."

"Ah, I see." For a minute Grandpa stared out over the lake. "Well," he began slowly, dropping the dug up plant into his bucket, "I do need to go over to Sunville and pick up some things." He squinted up at the sky. "You busy this afternoon?"

Liberty shook her head so hard her ponytail slapped her in the face.

"I'll call your mom, and if she agrees, and if Alec

wants to go, we'll leave right after lunch."

"Oh, thank you, Grandpa!" Liberty threw her arms around him and hugged him. "I just know he'll want to go! He's already been swimming with us twice, but of course we weren't really swimming, just playing in the water. Does he have to know how to swim before the parade?"

"No. But you'd better find him before he makes other plans." Grandpa returned to his search for trespassing dandelions, and Liberty ran to the house.

Bursting into the kitchen, she saw Grandma making lunch with Avery and Summer. "It smells good. What's for lunch? Where's Alec?"

"We're making cookies to decorate for the 4th, but we're having egg salad sandwiches for lunch," Avery replied, opening the oven door to check on the cookies. "I don't know where Alec is."

"Check on the front porch, Libby," Grandma suggested.

Skipping away, Liberty looked on the front porch and found Piper playing a game of Chinese checkers with Nan and Dory while Jainy pushed her doll in a stroller. There was no sign of Alec. When she asked the girls, they all shook their heads. No one had seen him for much of the morning.

After checking all the downstairs rooms and not finding her cousin, Liberty climbed the stairs. The door of his room stood wide open and she looked in. Alec sat at his desk writing something.

Suddenly feeling shy, Liberty knocked softly on the doorframe.

"Hi," Alec said, looking up with a smile. "What can I do for you, cousin? Do you need a pencil sharpened?"

Smiling at his reference to her favorite book,

Liberty shook her head. "No, I want you to go with Grandpa and me to Sunville after lunch. Will you?"

Alec looked surprised. "Sure. Where's Sunville and why are we going there?"

Liberty spun her flip-flop around with her toes. "Let's pretend we're going to China."

For a moment Alec's face was confused, then a look of suspicion crept over it. "Are you trying to tell me we're going on a boat ride?" His voice was accusing, but his twinkling eyes showed Liberty that he wasn't upset.

"Yes. But it will just be you and me and Grandpa. You don't have to worry about us knowing you are scared 'cause we already do. And it's okay that you can't swim yet. We always wear life-jackets on the boats." Her foot stopped moving and she looked at him. "Will you go?"

Drawing a quick breath, Alec nodded. "On one condition."

"What?"

"That you'll start teaching me about the 4th of July. I need something to help me understand it all. All I remember from school is that England taxed the tea, the colonists didn't like it and dumped it into the harbor, and then they went to war. I always thought that was a pretty dumb thing to fight over."

"It wasn't about tea. But I agree. I'll teach you, but it will be better if the others help too. You have to learn about the Revolution and the Declaration of Independence and the Constitution and the Amendments and the government of our country, and oh, there's so much! But you'll enjoy the 4th even better if you know all about it."

"I should hope so! All those big words make me feel

like taking a nap."

"It'll all make sense."

"Lunch!" Avery called up the stairs.

"Race you downstairs!" Liberty challenged, turning and rushing for the stairs.

Alec raced after her, and they both reached the kitchen at the same time, breathless and laughing.

When lunch was nearly over, Grandpa looked down the table to Grandma and said, "I'm going over to Sunville this afternoon, want me to pick up anything for you?"

"I don't think so. Are you going by yourself?"

"Nope. I'm taking a first and second mate along. Libby asked to go, and it's time Alec learned something about boats. No, girls," he said in answer to the instant pleas to go along. "I can't teach my second mate if I have a boat filled with passengers. Another time I'll take you all."

"I'm afraid I won't be much of a second mate, Grandpa," Alec said, accepting another sandwich from Grandma. "Better call me the cabin boy."

The phone rang, and Grandma left the kitchen to answer it.

"Do you get carsick, Alec?" Summer asked.

Alec shook his head. "Not'd I noffuf," he replied, his mouth stuffed with a bite he had just taken.

"Alec," Avery chided, "you're as bad as Nan. Summer would have waited for your answer until your mouth was empty."

With a shrug, Alec swallowed and reached for his glass of water. "I answered before I thought. When are we leaving, Grandpa?"

"Ten minutes."

Liberty was waiting on the back deck when Alec

came down. She looked him over carefully. He had his sunglasses on, wore a blue and white striped tee-shirt, and wore flip-flops on his feet.

Snapping to attention, he gave her a smart salute. "Cabin Boy Goldman reporting for duty, ma'am."

"As you were. You can wear tennis shoes instead of flip-flops if you want."

"I can?" Alec looked down at his feet. "How come you aren't?"

"'Cause I didn't bring mine. It won't matter though. There's Grandpa. Let's go."

"Aye aye."

Liberty, catching sight of a flag dancing merrily in the breeze, started whistling as they joined Grandpa and walked down the hill to the sandy shore and over to the boat dock near Main Street.

"What is that song, Libs?" Alec asked.

"*Hail, Columbia.*"

"Columbia. Is it a college song?"

Stopping in the middle of a bar, Liberty pushed her sunglasses up to her forehead and stared at him, her eyes wide. "College song? How would I know a college song?" When her cousin shrugged, Liberty shook her head. "It's a patriotic song. We'll have to add a list of those to what you need to learn."

Alec groaned. "I'm doomed to days spent at my desk, studying from sun up until sundown. Grandpa, send me back."

"Huh. No grandson of an Air Force man is a quitter."

"And no cousin of an Air Force brat is a quitter!" Liberty made a slapping sound with one of her flip-flops and pushed her sunglasses back down. "You've already conquered your dislike of cold water, and you're about to conquer your fear of boats. Then it will just be swimming–which can wait until after the Fourth–and all things American. Don't worry, Alec, we'll all teach you. Why, even Jainy can teach you some things. We have flash cards with the Amendments on them and she can drill you on those."

"Oh joy. Flashcards." Alec said the words so dolefully that Liberty burst into laughter and even Grandpa smiled.

"Forget all that now, Alec, because here we are." And Grandpa stopped before a good sized boat.

Liberty scrambled aboard right away. "Come on." She beckoned.

Staring, Alec took his sunglasses off as though they might be obstructing his view. "But, where are the sails?"

"Sails?" Grandpa echoed. "Son, this isn't a sail boat. This is a motor boat. Now climb in. I'll have you running her in no time. If you're wanting a sail boat you'll have to wait until your uncle Byron gets home, and maybe he'll take you around to see a buddy of his who has one."

"Daddy would rather have his airplane," Liberty explained as Alec stepped into the boat and tried to walk over to a seat, "than a sail boat, even if he does like to go sailing."

"All it took was one trip in the cockpit of a plane," Grandpa said, "and Byron was headed for the Air Force."

"Did Dad and Uncle Hunter ever try flying in the cockpit of an airplane, Grandpa?" Alec sat down and looked about him.

"Yep, but the bug didn't bite them. Now come over here and we'll get this thing going."

The trip to Sunville was a success in taking away Alec's fear of boats. Liberty was pleased about that, but she couldn't help wondering how to go about educating him in all the aspects of patriotism, American history, and the reason for celebrating Independence Day which were so dear to her own heart and to the heart of her family. Walking back to Grandma's she only sort of listened to Alec answering Grandpa's questions about what he did back home. Her mind was busy with other things.

"Libs," Alec said, putting his hand on her arm when they reached the deck. Grandpa had gone around to the garage to put away the parts he had gotten for his lawn mower, leaving the cousins alone. "Are you all right? You're not mad at me, are you?"

"Mad at you? Why would I be mad?"

"I don't know, but you haven't said much of anything since we left Sunville. Did I take your jobs on *The Patriot*?"

Liberty shook her head. "Yes, but I don't mind. I was just thinking."

"Did I pass my boating test?"

"Yep."

They heard Avery's voice inside. "Come on, girls. They're back and we have to leave." The back door opened and Avery stepped out. "We have to go home, Libs. Our AORs are waiting. Summer and Piper already left; we were just waiting for you to get back."

Nan and Dory ran through the back door and Jainy came trailing after them. "Bye Alec!" they called, skipping down the steps and rushing across the yard. Liberty only had time for a quick farewell before she ran after her sisters.

"Wait!" Alec shouted.

Liberty stopped to see Alec running after them. "What?"

"What are AORs? Is it something else I have to learn?"

Bursting into laughter, Liberty explained, "It's just an acronym for Areas of Responsibility. Like chores. Dad's called them AORs for as long as I can remember. But I'd better fly. See you!" And taking off her flip-flops, Liberty raced after her sister, her bare feet hardly seeming to touch the ground.

5.

College for One

That night Liberty stared up at the dark ceiling. "Avery," she whispered.

"Yeah?"

The two older girls shared a room, and it was at times like this that Liberty was glad she didn't have to worry about waking the younger girls. "How are we going to teach Alec about the 4th of July? He thought *Hail, Columbia* was a college song!"

"Oh, dear. We'll have to help him with songs. But doesn't he know what Independence Day is about?"

Liberty folded her hands under her head. "He knows it's when America broke away from England, but he thinks it was all about tea."

"And he thinks we'd fight a war just because someone taxed our tea?" Avery sounded incredulous.

"I know, it sounds silly, and I'm not sure if he really believes that or just doesn't really know. But how are we going to teach him? There's not a whole lot of time before the 4th."

"Well–" Avery paused. "He could read the Declaration of Independence."

"I don't think that will do much good. Wait!" Sitting up suddenly, Liberty turned and faced her sister in the dark. "What if we acted it out? Then he'd remember. And it would help the younger ones too. Don't you remember how Dad had us act out the Constitution and what it meant? Why not do it with the Declaration of Independence?"

"You mean like all the grievances and such?"

"Yeah. Don't you think that would help?"

"I'm sure it would. Let's talk to Mom about it tomorrow. He could also watch *A More Perfect Union* even if it is about the Constitution, and not really the 4th of July."

"Maybe we can have a movie night at Grandma's and all eat popcorn and watch it." Liberty lay back down and pulled the sheet over her. "And we'll have to have music practice." She yawned. "I wonder if Daddy would have any other ideas of how to teach him?"

Avery's voice was quieter, "I don't know, but we'll have to teach him before Dad gets home."

*

"Do you think it will work?" Summer asked.

The four older girls were sitting in the shade of a large tree in Summer and Piper's yard. Somewhere Nan and Dory were off playing, while Jainy had gone shopping with Mom. It was a warm sunny morning. There had been no sign of Alec, but the girls didn't care, for they were planning his education.

"I think it will," Avery said. "It helped us learn the Constitution and the Amendments."

"We just have to figure out how to act it all out,"

Liberty said, pulling a small book from her pocket which she set on top of *Eight Cousins*. It was the Declaration of Independence and the Constitution. "He might have the preamble memorized, but I don't know." She looked doubtful, for their cousin had shown a serious lack of knowledge in American Government and history. "He'll have to help us do it, or it won't mean as much."

"Why don't we ask him to help plan it?" Summer said. "That way he'll know it better."

"It might be kind of fun to practice it and do it on the 4th, don't you think so?" Piper, sitting cross-legged, looked around.

Liberty nodded. She had thought of that last night but wasn't sure the others would agree. "I think we should at least try for it."

"Try for what?" a new voice asked, and Alec appeared before them. He looked around. "Is this the Cozy Corner? And am I intruding?"

"No, you're not intruding," Avery said, motioning him to have a seat. "And it's not the Cozy Corner."

"It's a college," Liberty said, her eyes twinkling with fun. "A college for one."

"I have a strange feeling," Alec began, settling himself in the grass, "that I'm the only student and that you are the professors."

Piper grinned. "I think Avery and Liberty and Summer are the professors. I'm just an assistant."

"Ah. What's the lesson today? I've had swimming, boating, flag raising, and have learned what an AOR is. I think I'm prepared for something new." And Alec folded his arms and waited.

Liberty looked at her sister. What were they going to start with? "I think–" she began, but suddenly the others started talking too. Everyone had something to say, and no one stopped to listen to anyone else.

"Start your engines!" Alec put his hands over his ears. "I mean change it up! No, I meant cut it out, or . . . or help!"

Suddenly Nan's high voice cut into the babble of words. "Throttle back!"

The silence which followed was instantaneous, and Alec heaved a sigh of relief. "Thanks, Nan. I couldn't remember what to say to stop the flow of words. Throttle back. Throttle back." He muttered the words to himself.

"No problem," she said, sitting down. Dory sat down next to her. "What are we planning?"

"Avery, you tell," Liberty said.

"No, it was your idea."

Quickly, Liberty explained her plan, ending with, "You will help us, won't you Alec?"

"Sure. I did read the Declaration of Independence last night before bed. Not sure I understood it all, but I guess it was more than just a tax on tea."

"Of course it was!" Liberty picked up the small book. "It wasn't that the colonies just threw a tantrum because they didn't get their way once. King George III refused to treat them as Englishmen. He encouraged the Indians to attack the colonies, he captured men from ships and forced them to fight against their own families in the colonies! He sent troops against the people when nothing had happened, and there were even innocent men who had done nothing that were taken to England to be tried." Liberty was growing indignant. "Now, if that doesn't sound like good reason to protest, I don't know what does."

Avery picked up the lesson. "The colonies tried over and over and over to work things out, but England wouldn't listen. Our Founding Fathers knew that if something didn't happen we would lose our right to worship God freely, which is why the pilgrims came over here in the first place, and then things would just get worse."

"So," Summer put in, "they risked their lives, their fortunes, and their honor to create a country free from the tyrannical rule of such men as King George III."

Alec looked impressed. "Wow. I guess I was either asleep during history class or this wasn't taught."

"It could depend on what curriculum you used," Avery said. "But let's get back to our plan." She leaned back on her hands and stretched her legs out. "Libby?"

"I don't think we'll be able to act out the preamble," Liberty said, "but we could quote it and maybe parts of the next part before acting out the 'facts submitted to a candid world' as it says."

"We can act them out as someone quotes or reads them," Piper suggested.

"Good idea! If we all memorized one or two of them, surely we would have them all, right?" And Summer looked questioningly at Liberty who was busy counting.

"Twenty-seven. There are some really short ones that Jainy and Dory could memorize. Nan, you can learn some longer ones, can't you?"

Nan nodded quickly. "Can I have the one about ravaging our coasts and burning our towns?"

"Isn't there one about sending swarms of officers who ate up our substance?" Piper wanted to know. "It's fun to say 'swarms of officers'."

After quickly skimming some lines, Liberty read,

"'He has erected a multitude of new offices, and sent hither swarms of officers to harass our people, and eat their substance.'"

Alec shook his head. "I think we need a notebook to write down who is going to learn which grievance so we don't forget. I'm not the best memorizer, but I might be able to learn three or four."

Summer jumped up and ran inside, returning moments later with a notebook and a collection of colored pens. Alec took the Declaration of Independence and began reading it so that parts could be assigned.

"Libby, pick a part," Piper said, giving her a friendly push.

"I'll take any of them. But, guys, I was just thinking." The pen stilled and everyone looked at her. "You know, someone always reads the Declaration of Independence at the town celebration . . ." She looked around. "If we really learned it . . ."

"You want us to do this before the whole town?" Avery looked aghast at the very thought.

"Oh, it would be fun, Ave," Piper said. "It would help people remember it too, you know."

"There really won't be any other time to do it on the 4th since we're playing Patriotic Charades in the morning," Liberty put in. "Please, Avery!"

"Come on, Avery," Alec joined in. "It'll be fun. I want someone to record it so I can send it to my parents, and if we are doing it for everyone, we might have mics that would make it easier to hear."

"Please, Avery!" Nan bounced on her knees, her eyes pleading.

"All right. If they want us."

A cheer went up from the others, and Liberty

leaned over and hugged her sister. "It'll be fun!"

Avery didn't look too excited but said, "We'd better get to work if it's to be any good."

"Then let's scramble!" And Liberty tore a piece of paper from Summer's notebook. However, on seeing the blank look on Alec's face, she paused to explain. "When the Air Force pilots are told to scramble, it means the enemy is coming and they have to get to their planes and get ready to do their jobs in a hurry, so when we need to get to work in a hurry, we say scramble."

"Got it. . . . I think."

"Who's going to ask about us doing it for the celebration?" Piper wanted to know.

"Not me. It was Liberty's idea." And Avery looked at her sister.

"We'll have to check with Mom first, and we can't do that until she gets home. And Aunt Tessa and Uncle Hunter will have to approve too. Grandma and Grandpa won't care though." She wrinkled her nose in thought. "I don't think."

"Well, let's work on this now. We can ask later, because we need to learn it anyway." Summer began writing again.

6.

Sacrifice

They spent all morning on their project and went inside with hearty appetites. Aunt Tessa was in full support of their project.

"I'm sure Grandpa would take you down to see the mayor this weekend if you asked. But you'll have to really work on this since you only have two weeks."

"We can get it done, but," Liberty said, "maybe we should practice music after lunch."

"Music?" Alec looked interested. "What sort of music? As long as I don't have to play any instrument, I'm good."

Aunt Tessa laughed. "If this is a patriotic song practice, I'll play for you."

"Thanks, Aunt Tessa," Liberty said. "It is. Alec has to know the songs we'll be singing on the 4th since no one is given sheet music."

"How hard can it be?" Alec asked, accepting the extra grilled cheese sandwich and last apple slices. "I mean you sing the *Star-Spangled Banner*, *America the Beautiful*, and–" He held his sandwich in his hands and his eyebrows contracted. "There's one more. Can't think of the name of it though." He took a large bite.

"*My Country Tis of Thee?*" ventured Avery.

"Dosh eet."

The girls exchanged glances and then started laughing.

As soon as his mouth was empty, Alec looked around the table. "What's so funny?"

"There are more songs than just those three," Piper said.

"And do you know all the verses of our national anthem?" Liberty asked.

Alec stopped chewing a second and then swallowed his bite. "There's more than one?"

"There are four of them," Nan explained. "And we sing them all on the 4th."

"How many other songs are there?" Alec's voice was slightly worried.

"Oh, I don't know. But don't worry," Liberty assured him. "We'll help you."

Music practice did not go well that afternoon, for it was discovered that Alec was sadly lacking not only in words to the songs, but he was also unfamiliar with several tunes and could not remember which song went with which branch of the military. Finally, Aunt Tessa slid around on the piano bench.

"Okay, I think we've had enough learning for today. All of you run off and do something active and fun before Alec thinks we do nothing but study around here."

*

"Mom." Liberty wandered into what the girls called

"the library" that evening where Mrs. Goldman sat writing at a desk.

"Hmm," was the absent reply.

"Are you busy?"

"Just a minute, Lib." Mrs. Goldman rapidly jotted down some numbers and then turned and looked up at her daughter. "I think we'll be able to get some fireworks for when Dad's home." Her smile was bright.

Liberty's smile was half-hearted.

"What's the matter, honey?"

"Nothing really," Liberty began, spinning a flip-flop with her toes. "I was just wondering. Do you think it makes Daddy sad when he has to tell me he won't make it home for my birthday?"

Mrs. Goldman's eyes were soft. "I know it does, Libby. Your daddy wants so much to be home with you and the other girls, but his country needs him."

Giving a big sigh, Liberty nodded. "I know. I won't ask him anymore when he's coming home. I don't want to make it harder for him." She didn't add that it made it harder for her to hear the same answer. "Would he be sad to hear about all our plans for the 4th since he can't be here?"

Reaching up, Mrs. Goldman gently rubbed Liberty's arm. "Libby, your daddy wants to hear every single detail you are planning. It will make him feel as though he is a part of it, and he'll be able to imagine you doing all the things you tell him about. We'll take lots of pictures and videos so we can show him later. I know it won't be the same, but isn't our country worth a little sacrifice?"

A sacrifice. Liberty hadn't thought of it that way before. Couldn't she sacrifice a special day with her dad when the Founding Fathers willingly sacrificed their lives, their fortunes, and their sacred honor? It wasn't just something they had promised on paper in the Declaration of Independence, some of them had died because of the stand they had taken on July the 4th, 1776. Others had lost their homes, their health, their families. Was she strong enough to sacrifice just a little bit for her country? She nodded. "I'll tell him all about everything." She slipped her foot into her flip-flop. Thanks, Mama." Stooping a little, Liberty hugged her mom. "You're kind of like Aunt Jessie, you know. You are good at giving advice."

"Who?" Mrs. Goldman raised a questioning eyebrow.

"In *Eight Cousins*."

Shaking her head with a laugh, Mrs. Goldman turned back to her papers and numbers, waving her daughter away as she said, "Oh, no, I am NOT a book character."

With a smile and a lighter spring to her step than before, Liberty skipped from the room. "I'd better go find Jainy and help her learn her part of the Declaration of Independence. I really think she could have learned something longer than what we gave her, but that's all right. Someone has to have the shortest grievances." She pulled a paper from her pocket and murmured, "'For cutting off our trade with all parts of the world.' I guess I'll have hers memorized as well as my own."

Two weeks had seemed like plenty of time to Liberty when she first suggested presenting the Declaration of Independence to the town on the 4th of July, but the days were going by much faster than she had anticipated. Grandpa had taken her, Piper, and

Alec to talk to the mayor about their idea, and he was delighted with the suggestion and agreed to it at once.

After that Liberty worked as hard as she could to learn her own part and to help the others learn theirs, but it was hard. There were days when no one wanted to practice and everyone went swimming instead. One day Grandpa took everyone for a ride in the boat. They were able to practice singing then, but any attempt at getting her sisters or cousins to work on the other project was met with protests.

"I don't feel like doing it now, Libs."

"Not on the boat; we can't move like we are supposed to."

"Can't we just say the lines once through?" she had begged.

At last the older ones agreed to do it just once, but the younger ones had giggled and claimed they couldn't remember what to say.

Finally, Liberty had given up.

*

"Come on, girls," Liberty pleaded. "You have to memorize these." It was mid afternoon. The summer sun was hot, and Liberty, with her three younger sisters, was relaxing in the shade of a few tall trees. Nan and Dory were swinging in the hammock while Jainy used a stick to push herself back and forth in another swing. Only Liberty was stationary, sitting cross-legged on a blanket. "Now, let's go over them again. You have to know when you are supposed to say your lines."

"I don't want to practice," Dory said.

"Me either!" And Nan rocked the hammock like a boat. "I want to do something."

"We are doing something, Nan." Liberty began wishing Avery wasn't practicing the piano and could help her.

Another voice interrupted. "What are you doing?"

Liberty turned and saw Alec standing behind her with his hands in his pockets. "Hi. I'm trying to help the girls learn their parts for the 4th, but it's not working."

"Being difficult, are they?" Alec grinned.

"No," Jainy said, "we just don't want to practice now."

"Well," Alec said slowly, "if it's all right with Aunt Jo, could I persuade you to let your students off early, madam professor, and could I get some cousins to take a stroll with me?"

"Yes!" Nan jumped from the hammock so fast that she dumped Dory on the ground. "Where will we go?"

Shutting her small book, Liberty gave a sigh. They might as well stop, for no one was even paying attention to her now. She sat still and watched as Nan and Dory, who wasn't hurt from her tumble, grabbed Alec's hands and practically dragged him to the house while Jainy ran after them. If Alec hadn't come she might have persuaded the girls to go over their parts one more time. They only had one week left. Just a mere seven days. Or no, not even that, for they wouldn't practice on the 4th, she was certain of that. There wasn't much time. And tomorrow was Saturday which meant more AORs to do before they could even hope to practice. Perhaps they shouldn't have tried to do so much.

"We could have just told Alec to read the Declaration and the Constitution and taught him all four verses of the Star-Spangled Banner and said he was ready." She sighed again. It would have been easier, but her patriotic heart wouldn't consent to such half way instruction. Shifting her position slightly, she watched the flag on the flag pole flutter rather limply.

"Please be with Daddy," she prayed as she often did when watching Old Glory at the top of their flag pole. "Keep him safe, and please bring him home to us soon, Lord."

"Libby!" Avery's voice broke into her thoughts. "Come in and get your shoes on."

Reluctantly, Liberty rose and slowly walked to the house. "Why?" she asked her sister who was standing by the back door. "It's too hot for shoes and socks."

"Mom said if Alec goes with us we can walk on the streets down to The Big Dipper and get ice cream. Nan's calling Aunt Tessa to see if Summer and Piper can go too. Hurry and get your shoes."

The prospect of ice cream was pleasant, but it didn't lift Liberty's spirits much as she walked upstairs to her room. She felt sad and discouraged. They were going to look silly up on stage stumbling over their lines and coming in at the wrong time. "If only Daddy were here," she thought, pulling on her shortest socks. "He'd get them to working on it. I've tried being excited and enthusiastic, but that didn't work. I've tried making them work on it, but that didn't work either." Slowly she put on her shoes and began to tie the laces. "I'm afraid if I don't say anything, no one will even remember until the day before, and then we'll all be grumpy and cross."

As she walked downstairs and heard the excited chatter in the front yard, she felt like saying she wasn't going. She didn't feel like acting happy and excited.

Stopping, Liberty looked up at the picture of her

dad on the wall. His voice seemed to echo in her mind. "A pity party won't get the job done." His eyes looked right at hers. Somehow just seeing his picture gave her new courage. She straightened her shoulders and whispered, "I won't give up, Daddy. We'll get it done."

Marching into the kitchen, she grabbed her sunglasses and joined the others outside.

7.

Patriotic Pride

She didn't say anything as they hurried around the side of the yard and to the street. Streets and sidewalks did abound in Silver Lake, but the local residence seldom used them unless it was to go to church, or to a town not accessible by boat.

No one seemed to notice Liberty's silence, for Avery and Nan were busy telling Alec who lived in which houses, while Jainy chimed in her own remarks about anything, and Dory, by far the quietest of the girls, walked along and answered the few questions Alec asked her. Following behind, Liberty tried to think of a way that would motivate the others to learn their parts, but by the time they had reached Aunt Tessa's, and Summer and Piper had joined them, she still had no ideas.

"They just don't care," she thought to herself, blinking back the tears which insisted on rising. "I'm trying not to have a pity party, Daddy, but we have to practice!"

Suddenly she stopped short. Maybe it was time to appeal to their patriotic pride.

"Throttle back!"

Her shout made the others who were at least a house in front of her, stop short and turn. Folding her arms, she marched up to them, thankful they couldn't see the tears she knew were ready to spill over.

"Were we walking too fast, Libs?" Alec asked.

"No."

"What's the matter?" Avery shifted her weight from one foot to the other. "Can't we talk about it at The Big Dipper?"

"We have five days."

"Five days for what?" Piper looked confused.

"Five days to finish learning and polishing the Declaration of Independence."

"We have a week, Libs," Avery said with a sigh.

"No we don't. We have tomorrow." Liberty starting ticking off each day on her fingers. "We won't practice on Sunday, so that day is out. Then we have Monday, Tuesday, Wednesday, and Thursday. The 4th is on Friday. If we don't do some serious practicing and memorizing, we are going to be a disgrace to the United States Air Force and the United States of America! Daddy might not be there to watch us in person, but he'll see a video. Do we really want him to see us mumbling and messing up the words to one of the greatest documents of our country? Do we even care enough to put our hearts into learning it? Maybe I should tell the mayor that we can't do it. He'll have to find someone to read the Declaration like he always does. Then you can all forget about it."

Afraid to say more, and afraid she'd already said too much, Liberty walked around the others and started toward town alone. She would just talk to the mayor.

Steps pounded on the street, but Liberty didn't turn.

"I thought Air Force brats don't quit," Alec said as he reached her side.

"They shouldn't, but sometimes they do." She blinked quickly. "Sometimes they get shot down or their engines fail."

The others joined them, and Jainy slipped her hand into Liberty's. "Can we practice after we eat ice cream?" she asked, looking up.

Keeping her face forward, Liberty said quietly, "The others don't want to, Jainy."

"Hey," Alec said. "Who said we don't? I'll admit I haven't wanted to before. I didn't feel like working hard and learning things, but I never wanted to quit. I just like to procrastinate."

"Libby," Avery said, linking arms with her sister, "we're sorry. We should have worked on it sooner. I know you hate doing things at the last minute, but I kept thinking we'd have plenty of time. I guess we don't. You've tried to tell us we needed to practice, and if we mess up on the 4th, the blame rests squarely on our shoulders, not yours."

"Not sure how we're going to divide blame evenly on seven sets of shoulders and keep it square," Alec remarked.

Liberty felt a small hope begin to rise. "You all have to want to practice or it's no good."

"We want to."

"I have my lines learned, but not when to come in."

"We can practice after we get ice cream."

Liberty stopped and pushed her sunglasses to her forehead and looked around her. "You all really want to do this?"

"Yes."

Avery hugged her and whispered, "I'm sorry I

didn't help you before, but I will now."

"Thanks." Liberty returned the hug. "Let's go get ice cream."

The Big Dipper was a small ice cream shop well known in the area for its fabulous ice cream and large scoops. The owner, an older man who had served in the National Guard for over forty years, was everyone's friend and loved his country and his flag as much as the Goldmans did. When the cousins arrived, they found him setting a small American flag on each table.

He looked up with a smile. "Well, hello, and what can I get for you ladies and gentleman today?" He moved behind the counter.

Most of the girls had favorites and were served quickly. Liberty eyed the choices with care. She wanted something special. All at once her eyes landed on a flavor she'd never tried before. "Mr. Custis, what's in the All American?"

The older man grinned. "Vanilla ice cream with fried apples and cookie pieces. It's a softer ice cream."

"I want that."

Taking up his large scoop, Mr. Custis dipped it into the cold treat. The scoop was perfect as he pressed it into the red dish. He grabbed a spoon and stuck it in one side, but instead of handing it to Liberty, he reached under the counter and pulled out a mini flag and stuck it in the top of the scoop. "Can't have an All American ice cream served without a flag," he said with a wink as he handed it over.

Liberty took a bite and closed her eyes as the flavors of the cinnamon apples and the slight crunch of the cookies melted together with the vanilla ice cream. "It's perfect."

They all ate their ice cream sitting in a large corner booth while they took turns reading or quoting their parts of the Declaration. There was more laughter than practice, but somehow Liberty was sure they would really settle down to work afterwards.

She was right. With Avery and Alec setting examples of serious work, the others followed, and by the time they broke up for supper Liberty felt much better about the whole thing.

*

"Daddy," Liberty said, trying not to bounce on the couch where she was sitting, "we're going to say the Declaration of Independence on the 4th!"

"For the whole town!" Nan added.

It was Saturday afternoon, and the family was Skyping with Dad overseas. He had said he wasn't able to do it the next day, so the girls had gladly interrupted their practice to come inside and talk.

"Really? Just you five?" Dad's smiling face on the screen looked interested.

"No, Summer and Piper and Alec are doing it with us," Avery said.

"They're on the porch," Dory put in. "'Cause we were practicing."

"Aren't they going to come in and tell me hello?" Dad asked.

"I'll get them." And Liberty raced from the room. "Come in! Daddy wants to say hi," she called, shoving open the screen door.

Summer and Piper hurried inside, but Alec was a little slow. Liberty grabbed his hand and dragged him into the room. "Here's Alec, Dad."

Byron Goldman looked through the screen at the tall, lanky young man and smiled. "Hi, Alec. You look just like your dad. I hope you're not too overwhelmed by all these girls."

"No, sir. They're teaching me things about America and the 4th of July that I didn't know about."

"Oh, what sorts of things?" Mr. Goldman looked at the group of faces.

Those words released the dam, and all the girls began talking at once.

"Throttle back!"

The order brought instant silence. And then Liberty giggled. "We're still trying to teach that to Alec, Daddy."

Grinning, Mr. Goldman said, "He'll get the hang of it if he's around you girls long enough. Now, tell me what's planned for the 4th. And don't all talk at once."

Rapidly, Avery, Liberty, and Nan, with a few words from Piper or Summer, explained the schedule the town had released for the festivities. The boat parade was the first thing, followed by races and contests, and then a huge cookout with a patriotic program of music and speeches in the evening. The day would end with fireworks at night.

"But we're going to do Patriotic Charades in the morning, Daddy," Liberty said. "Just like we always do."

"Are you opening presents in the morning too?"

Liberty looked over at her mom and then shrugged. "I don't know."

"Well, I'll try to call or something that day. Not sure when though, all right?"

"All right." And Liberty smiled. It still hurt knowing that Daddy wasn't going to be home for her birthday, but she wasn't going to make him sad if she could help it.

"You all work hard and do your very best. I'm looking forward to hearing all about it. And I hope someone is planning on videoing your performance of the Declaration because I want to see it."

"Someone will."

*

Practices were going smoothly. Liberty wasn't sure if it was Dad's talk which had motivated the others to greater effort, or if they had just decided to buckle down and do their best, but whatever the reason, there was no more complaining about practicing. They even had time to work on music with Alec until he was at least quite familiar with such patriotic songs as *God Bless America, You're a Grand Old Flag, This is My Country*, and others. He only got mixed up a few times on which verses came next in *America the Beautiful*. But he had learned all four verses of the *Star-Spangled Banner* completely.

"You know, Liberty," Alec said one day, "I'm glad I came here when I did. I had wanted to wait until later in the summer, but Dad said I needed to experience a 4th of July celebration in the States. I thought he was crazy since I figured all people did was watch a boring parade, eat hot dogs, and shoot off fireworks when it got dark. Thanks to you, I've learned there's a lot more to it."

Liberty colored under his praise. "You're welcome."

"But say," Alec went on. "In *Eight Cousins* they spend the night camping on an island for the 4th of

July, don't they?"

"Yes?" Liberty wondered what her cousin was thinking.

"I heard Avery mention something about some movie on the Constitution that you watch around this time of year. Do you think we could watch it some evening and then camp somewhere? Not on an island."

"We don't have any tents, but maybe Grandma and Grandpa would let us have a movie night at their house and watch it. We do that sometimes and then spend the night." She frowned. "But you're not a girl."

Alec threw back his head and laughed. "No way! And I hate sleeping on the floor. I'll go sleep in my own comfortable bed, and you girls can sleep on the floor since we can't sleep outside."

Liberty grinned. "Let's ask."

Grandma agreed, providing it was all right with everyone else. "I'm not sure when you're going to fit it in though, Libby," she said. "You're already busy. And don't you have to decorate the boat too?"

"Yes, but not until the 4th. After Charades."

There was some discussion among the adults, but at last it was decided that the cousins could eat supper and have a movie night at Grandma and Grandpa's and spend the night on the third.

"Mom," Liberty begged, "can't I please come home and raise the flag on the 4th? I always do it on my birthday, and I want to raise our flag not Grandma's. Please? I want to do it for Daddy."

"Do you think you can get here in time?" Mom asked with a smile. "You'll probably be up late."

"I'll be here."

"All right then. It is your birthday after all. I'll meet you here at the flag pole, okay?"

"Thanks, Mom." Wrapping her arms around her mom, Liberty gave her a tight hug. "I love you."
"I love you too, Libby."

8.

Independence Day

Yawning, Liberty dressed as quickly as she could in her red, white, and blue star-spangled dress. She pulled her hair into a quick pony tail and then slipped into the kitchen. "Morning, Grandma."

"Good morning and happy birthday, Libby. Are the others up?"

"They're getting up. But I have to run home to raise the flag." She looked up at the clock. It was still early, but the flags were raised at dawn on Independence Day. "I should go."

"Let me call your mom and let her know you're coming," Grandma said, reaching for the phone. "Then you can just call before you start back, okay?"

Liberty nodded and yawned again. Last night had been fun. Everyone had relaxed on the couch and the floor with pillows and blankets and had watched *A More Perfect Union*. Jainy and Dory had fallen asleep before it was over, and even Nan had nodded off a few times. But the others had watched it all the way through and then had stayed up talking about it until well past ten-thirty. At last Grandpa, who had dozed in his chair, roused and sent everyone to bed.

Grandma hung up the phone and nodded. "You can go."

Not bothering to put on her shoes, Liberty slipped out of the kitchen, across the deck, and then ran across the green grass. It was almost scary running alone when the sun wasn't up, but it was also exciting. Today she was thirteen. Today was America's birthday too. "Happy Independence Day, Daddy," she whispered into the stillness.

Up ahead she saw Mom waiting by their flag pole. Light was glowing in the eastern sky. The bell would sound any minute. Quickly, she took the flag and clipped it to the rope.

"Happy birthday, Liberty," Mom said softly, letting the flag rest in her hands ready to be hoisted to the top of the pole.

"Thanks."

The bells began to ring and Liberty, with a strong hand, pulled the rope and raised the Stars and Stripes. A breeze off the lake caught the flag and set the colors rippling in the air.

Placing her hand over her heart, but keeping her eyes on the flag, Liberty began, "I pledge allegiance to the flag of the United States of America, and to the republic for which it stands, one nation under God, indivisible, with liberty and justice for all."

Mom dropped a kiss on her forehead. "I'm going to go inside. Are you coming?"

"Not quite yet."

Mrs. Goldman nodded and walked away.

Standing there alone as the light of the early morning spilled out over the sky and touched the clouds with pink and purple, Liberty watched the flag.

"Please, dear Lord, be with Daddy today even though it is almost night there. Please keep him safe and let him know how much I love him and miss him. And please, dear Jesus, bring him home soon."

"Liberty."

For a second, Liberty didn't move, then slowly she turned. By the dawn's early light she saw a familiar figure standing behind her. His uniform was only a dark shadow, but she recognized him instantly. "Daddy?" The name was a whisper. "Daddy!" With a cry she raced across the grass and flung herself into the open arms. Her legs wrapped around his waist and her hands gripped the back of his shirt. Tears ran down her cheeks, and she could hardly catch her breath as she buried her face in his shirt.

"Libby, I'm home."

But Liberty couldn't do anything except hang on tighter and cry.

Dad chuckled a little and hugged her close. "Hey, are you all right?"

"Don't wake me up. I don't want to wake up," Liberty said through her tears.

"You're not sleeping, Libs," Dad promised. "I'm really here."

"Are you sure?"

At that Dad laughed. "Positive, but if you don't stop half strangling me, I'll drop you."

Loosening her hold, Liberty lifted her head and looked at the smiling face she had so longed to see. "Daddy. You came home . . . for my birthday! I thought you couldn't come."

"I thought so too." Captain Goldman set Liberty down. "Let's go inside and find Mom."

Inside, Mrs. Goldman insisted on a picture of the

two of them. "Liberty, are you going to share your birthday present with everyone else?"

Liberty looked up at her father. "Do the others know you're here?"

"Only Grandma and Grandpa. They let you kids all spend the night so your mom could pick me up at the airport."

"You mean you were here all night?" When her parents started laughing, Liberty wiped the tears away and joined in. "Are we going to Grandma's for breakfast?"

"Yes. I got two of my girls back in my arms, but I'm still missing four of them." And Dad smiled from Mom to Liberty.

At Grandma's, Avery caught sight of them before they had reached the house. The others must have heard her for they soon followed, and the reunion took place in the grass under the flagpole. There was so much talking and hugging, and laughing that it was a little while before everyone managed to get back inside to eat.

"I thought you couldn't come until later, Dad," Avery said once everyone was eating.

"So did I. But I found out last week that we were headed Stateside on Sunday. That's why we had to talk on Saturday. I wasn't sure what we'd be doing when we got back to the States, or if I'd be able to get a few days of leave, so I didn't say anything. Turns out my CO thought I should be home for my daughter's thirteenth birthday since she shares a birthday with America, and after some phone calls with your mom, here I am."

After breakfast Grandma sent them all away saying that she and Grandpa and Alec would wash the dishes. Summer and Piper offered to stay and help clean up too.

Liberty couldn't help smiling at all the flags dancing in the breeze, at the red, white, and blue bunting hanging on porches and decks, and at the feel of excitement in the air. It felt as though everyone was celebrating with her. "Charades and then decorating the boat. You'll get to help, Dad!" She gave a little skip.

"When are you going to open your presents?" Dad asked.

"Oh, I don't care. Tomorrow or next week. I got the present I most wanted." And Liberty hugged her dad's arm and smiled up at him.

Once at home the family gathered for prayers and Bible reading. It was so good to have Dad back with them. Liberty kept looking over at him to make sure she wasn't dreaming, and the constant prayer in her heart was one of thankfulness for bringing her father home early.

Around eight-thirty Uncle Hunter and his family arrived followed shortly afterwards by Grandma, Grandpa, and Alec. The annual game of Patriotic Charades was played with equal enthusiasm by young and old alike. There was much laughter, some groans, and lots of cheering when a word or phrase was finally guessed.

"I'll have to catch my breath now," Grandpa said, leaning back in his armchair, "before I go decorate any boat."

"Oh, Daddy," Liberty turned to her father, "you'll help us decorate too, won't you?"

"I wouldn't miss it."

"In that case, Byron," Grandpa said, "you and Hunter take charge–I mean lend these youngsters a hand–with decorating, would you? I'd like to sit back and watch it happen for a change."

Captain Goldman looked at his daughters. "I assume you girls have the decorations all planned out?"

"Yep," Avery replied. "But a lot of it was Alec's ideas."

Liberty sprang up from the floor where she had been sitting. "Let's go decorate it now. It might take us a while even if we do have things planned."

The others rose too.

"We'd better take my truck," Uncle Hunter said, "since we loaded things in it yesterday."

Before long the decorating committee was climbing from the back of the truck near the dock. Only a few others were around to start decorating their boats, and Byron Goldman was greeted warmly.

"So, what's the plan?" Captain Goldman asked, putting his sunglasses on and looking around.

"We're going all out Air Force," Liberty said. "See, we got a lot of these foam planes and painted them. We're going to attach them to sticks and make it look like they are flying or taking off."

"Oh, so we're turning this boat into an aircraft carrier, are we? Are we leaving off the red, white, and blue decorations?"

"Of course not!" And Liberty looked shocked at the very idea. "It's going to have planes and bunting and flags."

"I assume you know where you want everything?"

"No, we just gathered the things," Avery admitted. "We didn't have time to figure out where to put it all."

"Then we had better get busy!" Captain Goldman began taking things from the back of the truck and handing them to the others to be carried to the boat.

Everyone set to work eagerly, and though things

were a little confusing at first, they soon began to take shape. Liberty found herself partnered with Piper in zip-tying American flags of all sizes to the sides of the boat and to the dowel-rods holding the planes up. Liberty smiled as she saw her dad and Alec attaching the small planes.

By eleven, the boat was ready and everyone put on their life-vests. Uncle Hunter took the helm, and the boat slowly joined the other boats, small and large ones, in one long line. The shores were crowded with people waiting for the parade to start.

The clear notes of a trumpet signaled the start and the crowds began to cheer.

"We won't go all around the lake," Liberty explained to Alec, "because it's too large, but we do go quite a ways. There are boats here from Sunville, so we'll go there. But we cut across the lake in the section where it's just woods and no people. Isn't this fun?" And Liberty waved to the people on shore.

"You don't get to throw candy or get any," Alec remarked.

Liberty laughed. "Who wants to? If you want candy, you can get it at the store. I wouldn't want any that had been in the street. That's just gross." And she wrinkled her nose while her cousin laughed.

When their boat finally returned to the dock, Liberty was happy to find her mom, aunt, and grandparents waiting with a quick lunch for everyone. After she had finished eating, she hurried back to the boat to start taking down the decorations.

As she was trying to undo a zip-tie, someone came up beside her.

"Want a little help with that?"

"Yes, please." Liberty smiled up at her dad. "I'm so

happy you're home," she whispered.

"I know. I'm pretty happy about it myself. Now, is there still going to be a three-legged race this year?"

"Uh huh." She took another flag and looked up. "You don't mind leaving Mom and the others just to do it with me?"

Dad pretended to frown. "Don't we always do the three-legged race together?"

Liberty nodded.

"Then why not this year? I'm not backing out. Besides, I hear your Uncle Hunter and Piper have been practicing. We can't let them win too easily, can we?"

Without thinking of the knife in her dad's hand, Liberty flung her arms around him, and only quick reflexes on his part saved her from cutting herself.

"Whoa there, Libs," he said, hugging her with one arm. "This knife is sharp."

"Sorry. I just–" Unexpected tears filled her eyes and one spilled down her cheek.

"Hey," Dad said gently, "no tears. I'm not mad at you."

"I know. I just had thought I wouldn't do the three-legged race this year because I didn't want to do it without you and–"

Dad's arm tightened around her shoulders, and he pressed a kiss to her hair. "Me too. Not that I was thinking of doing a three-legged race with any of my Air Force buddies . . ."

Liberty giggled at the thought of that, and the tears slipped back where they were supposed to be.

9.
How to Celebrate

It was an afternoon to remember. Liberty insisted on introducing Alec to all the contests and fun offered that day on the Silver Lake fair grounds. The rest of her cousins and sisters tagged along followed by the rest of the family. Alec was game to try almost anything from attempting to walk on stilts–which he eventually gave up on–to a watermelon seed spitting contest in which Liberty, Piper, Nan, Uncle Hunter, and Captain Goldman joined in. This proved to be somewhat easier, and Alec managed to hit the target twenty times and won an Uncle Sam hat which he insisted on wearing instead of the baseball cap over his blond hair.

A gunnysack race landed Alec face down in the dirt while Nan and Jainy hopped right past him.

"Don't say I'm not willing to get down in the dirt in order to celebrate America," Alec said, coming back spitting some grass out of his mouth.

"We won't," promised Liberty, laughing at the dirty smudges on her cousin's face. "Are you any good at catch?"

"Yeah. Why?"

"Want to be my partner for the egg toss?"

"The what?"

Captain Goldman clapped his hand on his nephew's shoulder. "The egg toss, Alec. If you take Liberty, you'll have a good partner. She's good at catching those raw eggs."

Alec's mouth dropped open. "Raw eggs?"

Bursting into laughter, Liberty grabbed Alec's hand and pulled him to the wide open space where the egg toss was about to start before he could back out. "All we have to do is toss an egg back and forth to each other without breaking it," she explained. "And each time one of us catches it, that person takes a step back."

"Is it really a raw egg?"

"Uh huh. So kind of move your hands back when you catch it or it will break." She tried to demonstrate with her hands.

"Okay," Alec still sounded skeptical. "And what does this have to do with the founding of America?"

"Nothing. But John Adams said that we ought to celebrate Independence Day with pomp and parades, games, sports, guns, bells, bonfires and fireworks. And this is a game." Liberty shrugged. "And it's fun. Who said all games have to be more than just for fun?"

Each team was allowed a second egg if theirs broke in the first three throws. Alec needed it after his first attempt at catching. After that he seemed to get the hang of it and cradled the egg as he caught it.

"Good!" Liberty praised. "Now we keep throwing and see how far apart we can get."

They both did their best and when their egg finally broke in Alec's hands, they found themselves in third place with only two other eggs still being tossed.

"That's because," Liberty whispered, "only two boys from the local baseball team entered. Usually there are several, and some of them just keep going and going."

Alec looked at his hands covered with raw egg. "Do I get to wash my hands, or must I wear egg on them for the rest of the day?"

Liberty laughed. "You get to wash them. But we have to get our 3rd place ribbons. They are just cheap ribbons, but if you have one and you stop at The Big Dipper and show Mr. Custis, you'll get a mini scoop of ice cream added to your regular scoop."

With their red, white, and blue ribbons around their necks, Liberty and Alec rejoined the rest of the family who cheered and congratulated them.

"It's almost time for the father-daughter three-legged race," Avery said, looking at her watch.

"Then we'd better head over there," Captain Goldman remarked, "because my partner and I have a race to win."

"Excuse me, brother," Uncle Hunter said, "but you don't stand a chance this year. Piper and I have been practicing."

Liberty and Piper exchanged grins. Their fathers were more competitive than they were. The summer sun was hot, but a breeze off the lake kept everyone from becoming overly warm and stirred the flags flying from every pole. Walking through the grounds toward the three-legged race, Liberty took off her ribbon and hung it around Dory's neck. "Hang on to it for me, Dory."

"Make a hole!"

Dad's sudden call sent the girls scrambling to the side of the dirt road. Liberty turned to see what was coming and saw Alec standing in the middle of the roadway with a confused look on his face. Before she could say anything her dad grabbed Alec's arm and pulled him back just as two boys on bicycles came racing by.

"They shouldn't be riding that fast around here," Grandpa said, his voice slightly stern. "I'm going to check into things."

Captain Goldman released his nephew's arm. "Sorry about that, Alec. I guess the girls haven't taught you about making a hole."

Alec shook his head. "Nope. I couldn't figure out what I was supposed to make a hole in. But I suppose it means get out of the way."

"Yep." Liberty looked up at her dad. "We've got to hurry."

Standing at the starting line with her left leg secured firmly to her dad's right leg, Liberty gripped a belt loop of his pants with her left hand and looked up.

"Ready?" Dad whispered.

"Ready."

The starting gun sounded, and Liberty took a step forward with her left leg. "In. Out. In. Out. In." She chanted the words matching each word with a step. She could feel her dad's arm around her. They were nearing the finish line and the cheering was getting louder. Where were Piper and Uncle Hunter? She didn't dare try to see them. And then there was the finish line. They were across!

Only then did she look around. To her surprise Uncle Hunter and Piper were still several yards away. When they finally came up, Liberty said, "Piper, what happened? You guys always beat us!"

"We weren't ready when it was time to start, and I got my feet mixed up and it took us time to get into rhythm again. But I'm glad you won if it couldn't be us." And Piper hugged Liberty.

There were more games and contests including a pie eating contest which Captain Goldman challenged Alec to join. It was a very messy contest, for no one was allowed to use their hands. The crowd cheered and shouted encouragement then laughed as pies almost fell on the ground or a contestant ended up with some cherry pie filling on his eyebrows. Alec did better than his uncle, but neither one came close to winning.

"Well," Alec exclaimed after he'd washed his face off and stood near Liberty again. "I never thought the 4th of July was such a messy holiday. Watermelon seeds, raw eggs, and now pie. What next?"

Laughing, Liberty handed Alec his sunglasses and Uncle Sam hat. "Just supper. The firemen cook up hot dogs and hamburgers for everyone, and there are chips and drinks and desserts from everyone. Remember all those cookies we helped decorate? Those were for this evening. It's kind of like a giant potluck supper only with everyone bringing just desserts."

"Wow. But I don't think I'm hungry."

"You will be later," Liberty promised. "You can't help being hungry when you smell the food cooking. Oh, we need to practice! Come on, let's catch up with the others and find out when we can."

Supper was every bit as good as Liberty had said, but the closer it got to the evening program, the more nervous she became. She handed the rest of her hot dog to her dad and her bag of chips to Alec. The practice for their presentation of the Declaration of Independence had not gone well. Dory had forgotten her lines completely, Piper and Nan had come in at the wrong times, and Alec had understandably fumbled through "He is at this time transporting large armies of foreign mercenaries to complete the works of death, desolation and tyranny, already begun with circumstances of cruelty and perfidy scarcely paralleled in the most barbarous ages, and totally unworthy the head of a civilized nation."

"It'll all come together just fine, Libs," Avery had tried to assure. "The last practice is always a mess."

"I didn't think I'd be so nervous," she admitted in a whisper. "But I didn't know Daddy was going to be here. I'm glad he is, but–"

Avery nodded. "I know. But we'll do fine. We have some songs to sing first and then we'll do it."

"Next thing you know," Alec put in, "it'll all be over."

Liberty gave a half-hearted smile. They were trying to help. Then her heart seemed to skip a beat as the mayor came over. She swallowed hard. The mayor stopped and shook hands with her dad, but she couldn't hear what either of them were saying. Dad was nodding. Was it about them? Just then Dad looked over at her and beckoned.

"Libs, are you up to helping me lead everyone in the Pledge of Allegiance?" Dad asked.

"Me?"

The mayor grinned. "I figure anyone who shares a birthday with America should be able to lead the Pledge of Allegiance."

"Well, Libs, you want to?"

Liberty looked up. "You'll help me?"

"Of course."

She nodded.

"Good!" The mayor said. "I've got the police

chaplain to start off in prayer, then you two for the pledge, and then some music before our special Declaration of Independence. I must say, Liberty, I'm looking forward to hearing this."

Liberty gulped.

"Well, folks, I must be off. We're starting in about thirty minutes." And the mayor hurried away leaving Liberty gripping her dad's hand in panic.

"We're not ready, Dad," she whispered. "What if we mess up? What if we can't remember anything?"

Captain Goldman crouched down and looked up into Liberty's troubled blue eyes. "You'll do just fine. Even Air Force officers are nervous when doing something for the first time."

Liberty looked doubtful. "You are?"

"Sure. Remember what Ben Franklin said? 'We must all hang together or we'll surely all hang separately.' Now, no one here is going to hang you if you mess up," and Dad winked, "but you've got to all work together and trust that everyone else knows what they are doing. And there's something else our Founding Fathers did."

After waiting a moment, Liberty realized her dad was waiting for her to answer. "Pray?"

He nodded. "Remember, the Bible say we can do all things through Christ. Why don't you round up the rest of the eight cousins and pray together?"

"I will. Thanks, Daddy!"

10.

Let Freedom Ring

Liberty tried to sing as she and her sisters and cousins waited off stage for their turn to go on, but her mouth felt dry.

"Libby," Dory whispered loudly, "I'm scared."

Alec leaned down. "Pretend you are doing it on Grandma's deck for your mom and dad. Everyone else is just a dandelion Grandpa hasn't dug up yet."

At that, Liberty smiled and felt herself relax. Nan giggled, and even Dory loosened her death grip on Liberty's hand.

Then it was time. The mayor introduced them. "We have eight cousins here who are going to give you a presentation of one of the most important documents in American history. It's the document which gave us our freedom to live, work, pray, and believe the way we feel is right. And now I'll be quiet and let the Goldman cousins take over."

Up on stage with hundreds of faces looking up at her, Liberty felt like her heart was in her throat. Then she remembered Dad's words. Even grown men got nervous.

"July 4th, 1776," Alec began the presentation.

"When in the course of human events it becomes necessary for one people to dissolve the political bands which have connected them with another, and to assume among the powers of the earth, the separate and equal station to which the laws of nature and of nature's God entitled them," These familiar words helped erase the butterflies Liberty still felt in her stomach. "–a decent respect to the opinions of mankind requires that they should declare the causes which impel them to the separation. We hold these truths to be self-evident, that all men are created equal, that they are endowed by their Creator with certain unalienable rights, that among these are life, liberty, and the pursuit of happiness."

The words rang out clearly from eight young voices. There was never a falter or hesitation.

". . . To prove this, let facts be submitted to a candid world."

Once the preamble was done, everyone became a little more relaxed because they could move and pretend when they weren't stating one of their grievances.

A chuckle ran through the crowd as Alec mounted some chairs at the far distant edge of the platform and beckoned the girls who hurried over and then had to totter on the edge of the platform as Summer quoted, "He has called together legislative bodies at places unusual, uncomfortable, and distant from the depository of their public records for the sole purpose of fatiguing them into compliance with his measures."

Liberty and Piper collapsed on the stage with sighs as though they were weary.

When Piper got to her line about "swarms of

officers to harass our people and eat their substance," the audience laughed, for Avery, Summer, Alec, and Liberty crowded around the three younger girls, pretending to pull their hair and eat their food.

And then it was the ending. All stood together and quoted, "We, therefore the representatives of the United States of America, in general congress, assembled, appealing to the Supreme Judge of the world for the rectitude of our intentions, do, in the name and by the authority of the good people of these colonies, solemnly publish and declare, that these United Colonies are, and of right ought to be, free and independent states; . . . We mutually pledge to each other our lives, our fortunes, and our sacred honor."

A thunder of applause rolled from the audience as the cousins finished the final words, but Liberty hardly heard them; she was looking at her dad. He was on his feet applauding with the rest, and the smile on his face made her sigh with happiness. They hadn't been a disgrace to their country.

The rest of the program was a blur to Liberty. She knew she sang more patriotic songs and watched a few skits about the founding of America, but now that their part was done, she suddenly felt tired. Sitting beside her dad, she leaned her head against his shoulder and let her body relax.

"I think someone's almost tired enough to skip the fireworks," Dad said, glancing down at her when the program was finally over.

Not moving, Liberty replied, "Almost but not quite."

"Do you still want to watch the fireworks from the boat? We could watch them from the hill where our flagpole is." Captain Goldman looked around at his wife and daughters.

Liberty sat up quickly. "We have to watch them from the boat. It's more fun that way. And besides, Alec has never watched fireworks from a boat before." She turned and looked at her cousin. "Have you?"

Alec shook his head.

Grandma spoke up then. "Well, Alec, you just go along with your cousins. Grandpa and I are going to watch them from our deck, but you should enjoy the full day." She looked at her eldest son. "You'll bring him home later, won't you Byron?"

"Of course, Mom." Captain Goldman looked behind him. "Hunter, you all joining us on the boat, or are you doing something else?"

"Oh, we'll join you."

Dusk was deepening into darkness as Uncle Hunter dropped anchor and killed the motor on the boat. A few other boats were riding at anchor nearby, but there was no shouting to each other or loud talking. Fireworks could be seen in every direction, for people were setting off their own before the grand display the town put on.

Liberty turned her head trying to see in every direction at once. She loved the fireworks almost as much as she loved the red, white, and blue of her country's flag. On one side of her, Dad sat with Jainy and Dory in his lap. On her other side sat Alec. The other girls were nearby, while Uncle Hunter and Aunt Tessa sat together and Mom sat on the other side of Dad.

"You know, Libs," Alec said quietly, "until today, I never really understood why Americans loved their country so much. But now, thanks to your college for one, I think I am starting to understand. I'm sure I have a lot left to learn though."

"Only the Constitution and the Amendments, and all about the wars," Liberty said cheerfully.

Alec shook his head with a smile. "I guess I won't graduate quite yet then. But seriously, Libs, thanks. Thanks for taking a cousin who hadn't a clue what the 4th of July really celebrated and making me eager to learn and serve this great country."

Captain Goldman looked over. "Ready to join the Air Force yet, Alec?"

"Daddy!" Liberty exclaimed. "He hasn't even been up in the cockpit of a plane!"

Alec smiled. "Not yet, sir. I think I have some more things to learn first."

Their conversation was interrupted by a cry of delight as the first of the large fireworks lit the sky.

Rockets whistled as they shot heavenward to burst in a brilliant show of colors. Some seemed to fall toward the earth in a shower of glittering light. Others exploded almost on top of each other in mesmerizing displays, while still others burst with more noise than lights, making the younger ones cover their ears.

Liberty didn't know how long the display lasted, but when a lull came before the grand finale, she said to anyone who would listen, "You know, we're ending the 4th just like Rose and Uncle Mac did in *Eight Cousins*."

Avery groaned. "Libby, I thought you'd gotten tired of that book."

"Tired of *Eight Cousins*? How can I, Avery; we are eight cousins."

The explosions, whistles, and glorious light display of the grand finale interrupted further talk.

When it was all over at last, Liberty gave a long sigh.

It was over. Oh, she knew people would continue to shoot off fireworks until midnight at least, but for her, America's birthday had been celebrated as John Adams would have liked.

"Happy birthday, America," she said. And then, because she just couldn't help it, she began to sing.

"My country, 'tis of thee,
Sweet land of liberty,
Of thee I sing;"

The others joined in.

"Land where my fathers died;
Land of the pilgrim's pride;
From ev'ry mountain side
Let freedom ring.

My native country, thee,
Land of the noble free,
Thy name I love;
I love thy rocks and rills,
Thy woods and templed hills;
My heart with rapture thrills,
Like that above."

Voices took up the song from the other boats, and the music seemed to echo across the water where those on shore joined in until it seemed as though the whole countryside was singing.

"Let music swell the breeze,
And ring from all the trees
Sweet freedom's song;

Let mortal tongues awake,
Let all that breathe partake;
Let rocks their silence break,
The sound prolong.

Our fathers' God! to thee,
Author of liberty,
To Thee we sing;
Long may our land be bright
With freedom's holy light;
Protect us by Thy might,
Great God, our King."

If you have enjoyed this story, please consider leaving
a review on your favorite book site or blog. Reviews
are an author's best friend and are like chocolates; you
can never have too many.

ABOUT THE AUTHOR

Rebekah A. Morris is a homeschool graduate, an enthusiastic freelance author and a passionate writing teacher. Her books include, among others, *Home Fires of the Great War*, *The Unexpected Request*, *Gift from the Storm* and her best selling *Triple Creek Ranch* series. Some of her favorite pastimes, when she isn't writing, include reading and coming up with dramatic and original things to do. The Show-Me state is where she calls home.

Find out more about this author and her other books and stories by visiting her website at www.readanotherpage.com.